Shoo Wee
MONKEY

T.W. HOLT

Print information available on the last page

To order additional copies of this book, contact:
Xlibris
1-888-795-4274
www.Xlibris.com
Orders@Xlibris.com

This book is dedicated to my
mom, dad, brother and sister.
Also to my favorite 3 little monkeys:
Charlie, Friday, and Ben.

Once upon a jungle night there
was a monkey. He was sleepy and
ready for bed.

But when he went to give his jungle
momma a goodnight kiss she said.

"SHOOWEE MONKEY!

You are SO stinky! What did you do all day?" she asked.

"Welllll" the Shoowee monkey said. "I..."

"Jumped for bananas, and then jumped higher.

Rolled in the dirt,"

"and played with the tigers!"

"I ran with the elephants and their
so long trunks."

"Then swam with the Hippos and almost sunk!"

"I played all day." said the Shoowee monkey. "Now I think it's time for bed."

"I DON'T THINK SO!" His jungle
momma said.

"It's time for a bath you Shoowee monkey."

"But momma," he cried. "Baths are NO FUN!"

He kicked and he screamed all the
way to the tub.

"Baths are no fun! I don't wanna scrub-a-dub!"

"Baths are to fun," His momma replied. "More fun than the jungle if you give it a try."

"Well..." thought the monkey. "I guess I can try."

"Good!" said jungle momma. "I hoped you'd say yes, because jungle bath times are THE VERY BEST!"

"You can...

Swim like a crocodile if you must ask."

"Wear all the bubbles in a big mustache!"

"You can splash so high,

And sink so low."

"Scrub-a-dub your ears,

And scrub-a-dub your toes!"

"You're right momma!" The Shoowee monkey laughed.

"All Shoowee monkeys have to take a bath!"

CPSIA information can be obtained
at www.ICGtesting.com
Printed in the USA
BVHW020825250619
551795BV00025B/65/P